I can't BEAR it!

Written by Carrie Hennon

Illustrated by Barbara Bakos

Licensed exclusively to Top That Publishing Ltd
Tide Mill Way, Woodbridge, Suffolk, IP12 1AP, UK
www.topthatpublishing.com
Copyright © 2016 Tide Mill Media
All rights reserved
2 4 6 8 9 7 5 3 1
Manufactured in China

ISBN 978-1-78445-589-7

A catalogue record for this book is available from the British Library

For Mila Beau Eve Hennon.

This is

Clare.

She might look like a sweet little girl ...

... but sometimes she can be a real

GRUMP!

This is

Bear.

When Clare doesn't want to do something she yells,

'I can't BEAR it!'

That's when Bear steps in.

'BEEP! BEEP! BEEP!' went the alarm.
It was time to get ready for school.

'First position please girls,'

said the ballet teacher, as the dance class began.

'I can't BEAR it!' complained Clare.
'I'd rather fly my kite.'

'Screech! Screech! SCREECH!'
went the violins in the music lesson.

'I can't BEAR it!'

yelled Clare.
'I'd rather listen to my own kind of music.'

'Lunch is ready!'

called Dad,
as he put a bowl of crunchy green salad on the table.

'I can't BEAR it!' moaned Clare.
'I'd rather eat a big slice of pizza.'

'On your marks,
get set, GO!'

started the three-legged
race on sports day.

When Mum asked Clare to tidy her room,
all Clare heard was, 'Blah, blah, blah!'

'I can't BEAR it!' sighed Clare.

'I'd rather play video games.'

'Come on Clare, it's time to help with the washing up,' called Mum.

'I can't BEAR it!'
grumbled Clare.
'I'd rather watch cartoons.'

'Come and give me a kiss, dear,'
said Grandma, as she puckered her lips ...

'I can't BEAR it!' shrieked Clare.
'I'd rather kiss the dog.'

And so things continued ...

Every time Clare didn't want to do something, poor Bear had to take her place.

'BEAR?!'

Until one day, Bear was nowhere to be found ...

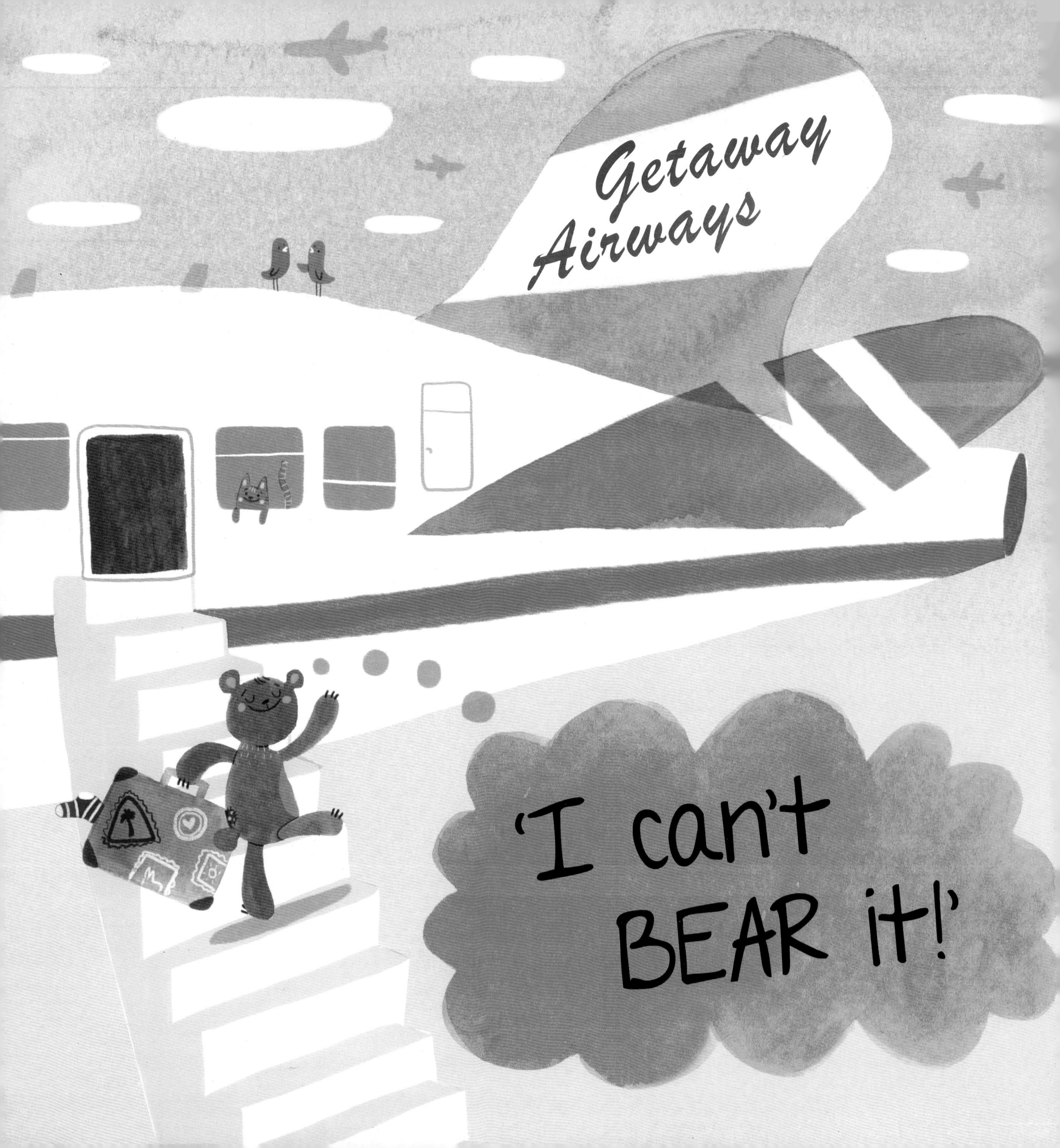
Getaway Airways
'I can't BEAR it!'

Ben's Counting Walk

ISBN 0-7696-4178-4

50395

9 780769 641782

EAN

Ben's Counting Walk

By Gill Matthews

Illustrated by Belinda Worsley

GINGHAM DOG
P R E S S

Columbus, Ohio

Ben and Sam went
for a walk.

Ben took his bag.

6

7

Sam did, too.

They found one wet worm,

10

two tiny tadpoles,

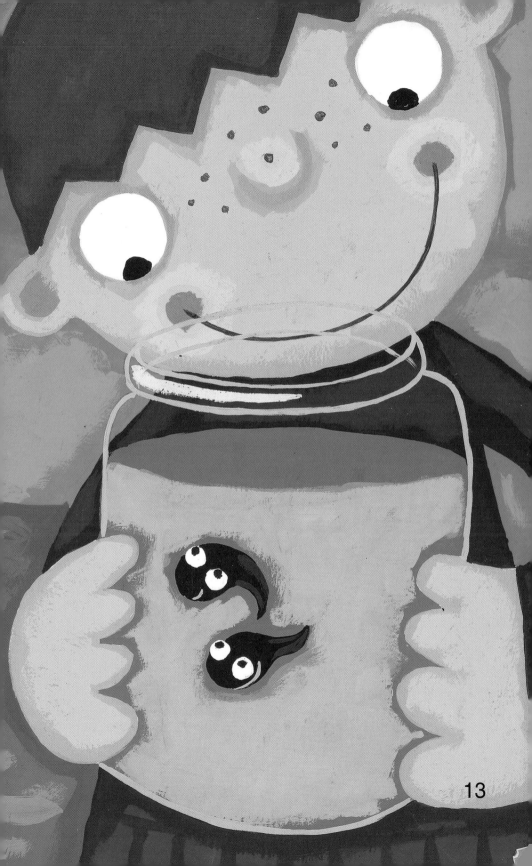

13

three thorny thistles,

14

15

four fat frogs,

five fine flowers,

six smooth stones,

20

21

seven slimy snails,

eight awesome apples,

nine neat nuts,

26

27

and ten tired toes!

28

Now, let's eat!

31

Words I Know

found   they

his   walk

bag   tired

now   went

Think About It!

1. What did Ben take with him on the walk? What did Sam take?

2. What was the first thing that Ben and Sam found? What was the last thing?

3. What did Ben and Sam do after the walk?

The Story and You

1. Do you like to take a walk with your family? Where do you go? What do you see?

2. Pretend that you are Ben. What are some other things you might have seen on your walk with Sam?